THE APPLE GUARDIAN

NATALIE ANNE DUTRA

outskirts press

This is a work of fiction. The events and characters described herein are imaginary and are not intended to refer to specific places or living persons. The opinions expressed in this manuscript are solely the opinions of the author and do not represent the opinions or thoughts of the publisher. The author has represented and warranted full ownership and/or legal right to publish all the materials in this book.

The Apple Guardian

v2.0

Bible references:

- Revised Standard Version
- Century King James Version
- New International Version
- New English Standard Version
- English Standard Version
- King James Version
- American King James Version

Outskirts Press, Inc.
http://www.outskirtspress.com

ISBN: 978-1-4787-7860-8

PRINTED IN THE UNITED STATES OF AMERICA

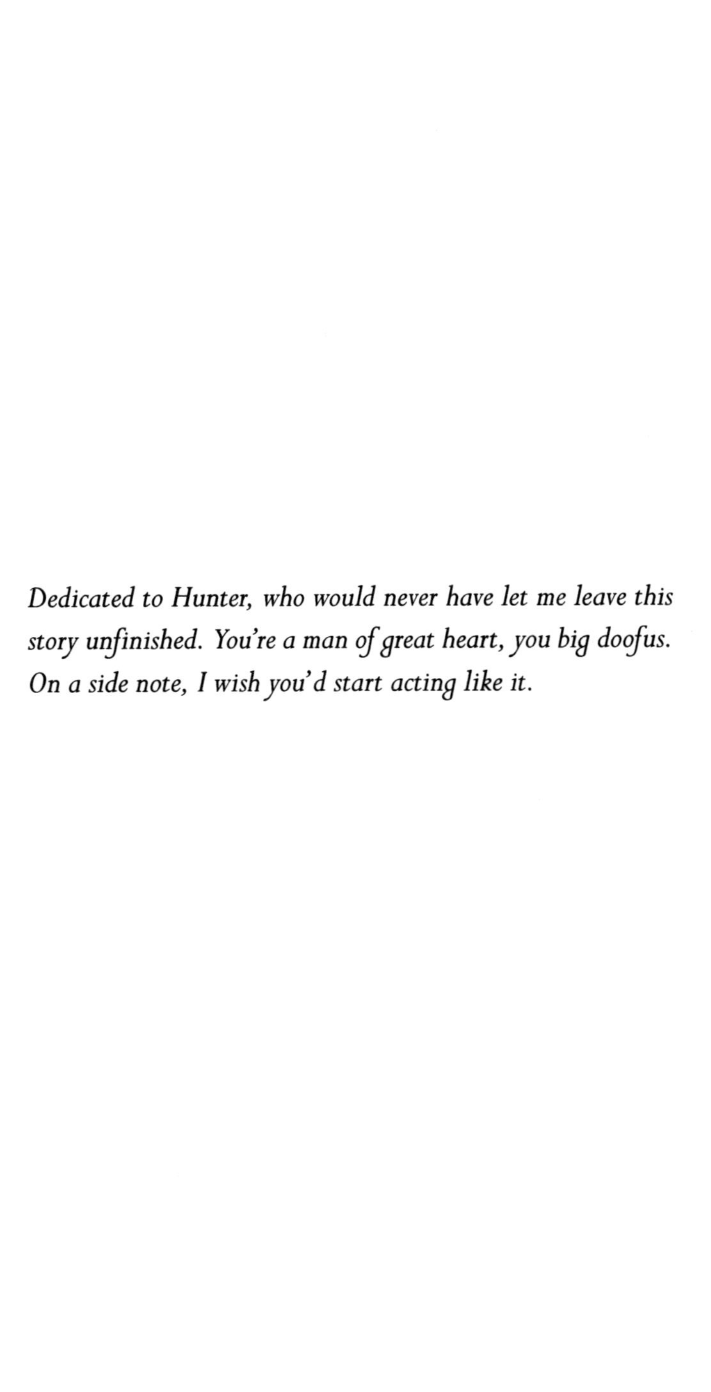

Dedicated to Hunter, who would never have let me leave this story unfinished. You're a man of great heart, you big doofus. On a side note, I wish you'd start acting like it.

Contents

Acknowledgements

First and foremost, I have to thank the three most important things in my life: the Father, Son, and Holy Spirit. I have no idea why I was blessed with a story to tell and I do not in any way deserve the adventure it's taken me on. My faith has brought me through some dark nights and rough waters, and I owe God more than I can ever repay. I pray that this deranged little story of mine will spark some deeper reflection on the legacy of Christ—or at least a bit of curiosity into the biblical references.

Next, I would like to thank my family. Mom, Pops, thank you for never giving up on me, even though it's taken me five years to write this tiny little something. Brian, thank you for inspiring the concrete half of the plot, which I managed to turn into something completely abstract like the true weirdo I am. Eric, thank you for motivating me to stick with my craft. I have to thank the Youngs for being my cheerleaders throughout this drawn-out writing process. Skylar, thank you for pestering me to keep writing and never giving me any actual feedback. Hunter, thank you for giving me feedback and being particularly enthusiastic about this story, even when I temporarily abandoned it to start other projects. Many thanks to both of you for believing in my writing.

And now, Thomas. You've always encouraged me in whatever endeavors I've pursued, and for that I will be forever grateful. You are the love of my life and I am overjoyed to have your support in what I love to do.

This one may seem a bit out there, but I'd finally like to thank William Shakespeare. While sitting in honors freshman English one day as a high school student, watching a documentary on your life and work, a vivid image inexplicably formed in my head of a wolf standing beneath an apple tree, which I proceeded to sketch in black pen on a piece of binder paper. I labeled it "Lazarus, the Apple Guardian" in the same sitting. This single drawing became the base for the entire abstract half of this story's plot, and came seemingly out of nowhere.

I will say, before I finish, that this story as a whole is not meant to be a biblical allegory. There are biblical elements and references, but there is a subtext of social commentary and the question of morality at play here as well, alongside more big-picture themes. For any who will be offended by rough language, I apologize in advance. However, I'd like to point out that every man has his demons and his quirks. These are what make beautiful the human experience. If I am at fault for creating an imperfect character, so be it. None of us alive and breathing is a perfect character, for there has been only one, and I refuse to feel ashamed for writing earnestly.

Part I

"But nothing unclean shall enter it, nor anyone who practices abomination or falsehood, but only those who are written in the Lamb's book of life."

—Revelation 21:27 (RSV)

The rich darkness engulfing me begins to part. Thick silence runs into distorted external noise, as when trembling hands muffle sobs. Now the black suddenly fades away, sending artificial light seeping into my dilated pupils. I blink. I weakly lift my head from where I lie to survey my surroundings. Wavering in and out of focus, my eyes start to ache. A sharp pain in my temple orders me back down to my pillow. All I've been able to collect is an image of a woman dressed from head to toe in the color teal. The only detailed feature I can make out is her striking scarlet lipstick. I see the corners of her mouth rise slightly, and now the teal woman with red lips is smiling at me.

My aching head throbs. My vision falters and dizzies me. Within the next few seconds, my eyelids have fallen shut, imprisoning my anxious curiosity. I surrender to sleep to defend myself from the void, but my fragile state of consciousness does not remain stable. Because only a fraction of mine is real, restful sleep, my dreams are short and sporadic. I long to rewind them; I long to relive those precious moments within the safe, secure confines of my own imagination, but I will not be graced with the privilege. No, I instead gain my awareness back and seize the chance, jolting myself upright and making my flimsy mattress quake. I must look something awful, something primitive, as I gasp for air with bulging eyes. I steady my breathing and slowly pan the room. All the walls, the floor, everything seems to be the same dull, pale-green color.

I inhale deeply for a sigh of relief, but end up choking on the sterile stench that only a hospital can produce. My face involuntarily twists into something I'm sure is grotesque. Soft, melodious laughter breaks out from my left and seems to bounce back off the bare walls to ring louder. I turn my head hesitantly. *The teal woman with red lips.*

"How you feeling, Skye?" the teal woman hums, her voice like velvet when she speaks. My own name turns over groggily in my mind, now just a foreign word. I make a sound that is half-chuckle and half-snort.

"I feel about as damn good as any man who's woke up in the hospital not knowin' why," I retort, my words slurring a bit. The woman maintains an unflinching smile as she continues.

"Now, now," she says. "That's no way to treat your nurse. It's my job to get you out of here, isn't it? Have some faith; it does wonders!" As she finishes, she lets a giggle slide through her lips.

Oh God, I think to myself. *Who does this lady think she is? Oprah?* I snicker and shake my head.

"Right," I say. "Hey, would you mind bringing me a glass of water? All this unconsciousness has me parched."

The nurse seems to be overjoyed at my request—I suppose because she's got nothing else to do at the moment—and eagerly shuffles through the door. It shuts with a click behind her and all at once I'm alone again. I observe the room more meticulously from where I lie and find several oddities about it. There is no TV in my room, perhaps due to lack of funding or whatever else the establishment's lousy excuse may be. Also, I take a mental note of the fact that I am not sharing my room with any other groaning, unfortunate victims of circumstance. The silence tempts me to fall asleep, but is in no way reassuring. From far off, I hear the faint hiss of a pipeline carrying water. *If you were set on tap water, why not get it out of the bathroom that's right damn here?*

The most peculiar thing by far that I am able to notice while the nurse is still outside, is the room's lack of adequate windows. By that, I mean that the room has a total of zero. This must be why the light seemed so surrealistic when I first opened my eyes.

Although the god-awful lights that cover the whole ceiling cause me to blink uncontrollably, I catch sight of a small nightstand-looking thing beside my bed. Two books, ripe with age but in excellent condition, lie neatly stacked beside a lamp that appears more than a little out of place, with floral patterns decorating the shade on each side. *'Cause I need some light to go with my light… Morons.*

I snarl at the lamp, disgusted. Still it stands unflinchingly. Out of sheer curiosity, I reach out a hand and switch the thing on. A perfect beam of dim, rosy warmth escapes from every flat side of the lampshade--a beautiful sight to behold, I'll admit. This simple change in lighting even does the sickly, nail polish-green walls some justice. But my awe is short-lived. I can again hear the clack of heels on uncarpeted floors approaching quickly. I hurriedly turn off the lamp, to shield its beauty from undeserving eyes.

"Here we are, Mr. Braxton," the teal woman chirps, a ridiculously overzealous smile splitting her face. I can hardly suppress the urge to vomit.

"Why, *thank* you, Miss," I play along cheerfully. "I'd tip you, but I don't have my wallet on me."

"Oh, Skye—what a card you are! *Surely* you must be feeling a bit better," she chuckles.

"Better than being unconscious? God, I *hope* so!" I finish, sending her into a fit of giggling that refuses to stop even as she changes my morphine drip. *And just for that, you'll be going home to a Corvette and a fully renovated house—I'll even pay your bills for the next thirteen years!*

I listen for the spiel, but nothing breaks the silence once her laughter subsides. *Huh. Oh well.*

I open my reluctant eyes again. My guess is that it's been at least a few hours since the teal woman was last here. I remember vaguely the expression on her face as she replenished the source that relieves my anguish. After she finished her phony-baloney-Miss-America-laugh, her face seemed to harden. *Maybe I'm lucky and I'll be able to get away with dying on morphine...*

And then I realize that the throbbing sensation in my head has returned to change my mind. *Wishful thinking.*

There are two light switches beside the room's entrance, and as I squint and blink to see further in the artificial light, I can tell that one of them is switched on and the other off. I look up grudgingly.

That plastic-coated, good-for-nothing airhead... The teal woman has left the set of lights directly above my space blazing down on me, and the ones on the opposite side of the room are off. The light blinds me; it strangles me like a pair of hands. I feel as though a sack of rocks is repeatedly being dropped on my skull. My eyes ache the same whether I open or close them. And above all, I am too weak to shout for the teal woman to come and rescue me.

To me, it feels like both Heaven and Hell are clashing to take hold of my mind, and what's left of my sanity—Heaven to preserve and nurture it, and Hell to capture and destroy it. *Who will win? Hellofagame.*

I guess I've been too entranced in my own agony to hear her ruby-red heels click-clacking down the hall, but the silky voice of the teal woman calls me back to my hospital bed.

"Skye..?" she questions ever-so-gingerly. "You alright, honey?" *Fan-fuckin'-tastic. Pumpkin.* I shake my head as slowly as possible, trying not to agitate it.

Though I figure I must be wrong, she gives what looks to me like a smirk. *Oh, you are* definitely *not Oprah, sugar.* Without another word, she walks over nonchalantly and adjusts my morphine again. Once I can feel it coursing through my veins, I smile blissfully.

"There you go," she cooes. Her voice alone is like

an extra dose—so downy, so sugar-coated. So...hopeful.

"Ahh," I start. "Thanks. I'm finding that lately, asleep is the best place to be." She displays a genuine, bittersweet smile at my words.

"Well Skye, in your condition, it's the best place *for* you to be," she says. I look at her quizzically. "I still haven't told you what you're in here for, have I? Oh! Silly me! You've suffered a serious concussion, you see. Quite frankly, I'm impressed by your level of awareness right now. You're *extremely* lucky, actually—the doctor has told me that you've managed to retain your long-term memory. It was quite a nasty wreck you were in... very tragic."

I blink dazedly, then find that my mouth is open and have to use my hand to shut it. I've heard of plenty of run-of-the-mill concussions before, but a serious concussion? *As in* severe? *How am I even thinking right now?*

"W-wait..." I stutter. The heavy unawareness of the morphine is beginning to fall over me like a toxic rain. "When... when was the assident? Whahappened?"

The teal woman seems amused by my slurring, and simply says, "Rest up, Skye. You need your strength."

The teal woman wins her way once again. Too bad for her, throwing me into artificial sleep doesn't stop my mind from racing. Doubtful, frustrated thoughts violently flash through my head. They prevent me from sleeping soundly, yet the drug overpowers what is natural and forbids me from gathering enough energy to rise. I am trapped. I am also a morphine junkie, however, and to my dismay/relief (pick your favorite), my willpower is losing to my willpower.

Part II

"And when He thus had spoken, He cried with a loud voice, 'Lazarus, come forth!'"

—John 11:43 (KJ21)

All of a sudden my eyes are open. There is no pain, no stale air in my lungs, no needles in my veins. I look down and find that I'm standing up. Sunbathed summer grass warms my feet and tickles my toes. I examine the world around me curiously, noting a lush overgrown field that seems to stretch endlessly in every direction. I raise my head and an instinctive hand flies up to shield my eyes from the clear flood of light cascading over this meadow. The sky, possibly the most peculiar feature of my surroundings, is a solid gray-purple hue, always constant, always unchanging. Not a cloud stains its mystery.

Off to my right, the landscape remains the same as far as the eye can see—save for a lone horse, fully tacked and riderless, staring back at me from about a mile off. It seems disoriented, lost…desperate. It's alone in such a tranquil place, yet its body language sets off the hair on the back of my neck. My pulse quickens and I get the faint upset of fear in the bottom of my stomach. I turn to walk in the opposite direction and am somewhat startled by a glorious apple tree I haven't previously noticed, only about a hundred feet from me.

Its leaves glisten like emeralds in the sunlight, unscathed and untouched by the passing of time. The tree bears only one apple, and it dangles from the lowest hanging branch. However, the sheer size of the tree keeps the delectable jewel just out of anyone's reach. Beneath the tree a large, oddly-shaped rock sits planted in the grass. The sides are jagged, like any ordinary rock, but the top is conveniently flat and smooth. This would explain the creature sleeping atop it—a magnificent silver wolf. I approach the tree cautiously, mesmerized by its beauty.

"Curiosity killed the cat, Skye Braxton," a grisly old voice snarls at me from behind. I feel the dusty, feverish breath of neglect on my shoulder and whirl around only to hear hoofbeats dash behind me once more. I spin around several times and the repetitive pounding of hooves on dirt still seems to be circling me. My dizziness and horror drop me to the ground, where I cover my ears. *I've lost my mind.* The dreadful noise stops abruptly and all is calm once more, so I hesitantly remove my hands from my ears and look up towards the apple tree. No movement from the wolf. I sigh in relief.

I slowly push up from my fetal position and brush myself off. Determined, I press onward towards the apple tree. A soft serenity seems to envelop the small patch on which the tree and great beast lie. As I begin to approach the tree, trying my best to tread lightly as I pass the solitary wolf, I hear a new voice from behind me. This one is a calmer, more collected voice—I can tell by its mercury-smooth sound that the owner has its head screwed on straight.

"Pity, really—that psychotic nag. Been out of his right mind ever since the day."

I spin around to find the wolf fixing one eye on me, still heavy with sleep. It yawns and stretches casually upon its perch, then gracefully leaps to the ground. Its coat gleams like a diamond, rippling along to the effortless movement of its muscles. It dips its head at me politely. "Much obliged, my friend. You've woken me from my comatose sleep. It sure gets dreary after twenty-nine songs." I blink.

"Oh, where are my manners?" At this, the wolf turns away from me and begins to circle the tree as he speaks. "I have many names. Hallucination, Madness… I've even been called the Mourner of Humanity…" Here he pauses and gazes dissatisfied at the single apple on the tree. "You, child of destiny, may call me Lazarus, the Apple Guardian."

"The... Apple Guardian?" I ask.

Lazarus breaks his intense stare at the apple and looks back at me, a glint of disappointment in his eyes. "Aye, Mr. Braxton. The Apple Guardian. I have been dreaming of this apple for the last twenty-nine songs, you see. I have been dreaming of nothing but reaching for it repeatedly and never quite grasping it. And here it is right before my eyes—oh! I should have been called Tantalus. But no, this tree must need a name as well, and she is such a beauty I wouldn't dare appoint her with such a masculine title. So then... Her name shall be Aglaea, for her splendor is yet unmatched by any other! Truly, I have seen no other tree in all my days quite so lovely as she..."

I let alone the fact that he can't have possibly seen any others before, if he's lived out his entire life on this lonely little patch.

"Listen, Lazarus... this has all been wonderfully strange and everything, but where exactly is the exit? Is there like, some magic portal or something that'll get me out of here? Here being...wherever it is we are..."

Lazarus looks at me skeptically like I'm the crazy one, his soft sleepy eyes suddenly gone cold. "Circle that rock four times tracking left, then walk straight back to the tree and place your right hand on the trunk. If ever you may need a cross word or sarcastic remark, please, don't hesitate to come back. And good day, sir." He irritably flicks his tail and steps back onto his rocky pedestal. He proceeds to curl up as dogs often do before sleep and tucks his paws and muzzle in facing away from me.

"Wait, Laz—" I begin.

"Good *day*, sir!" Lazarus cuts in, finishing our short introduction. All at once I regret interrupting him. He seems so content, like he already has everything together and there's nothing he bothers troubling himself with anymore. I feel a pang of jealousy for the serene life he leads, never having to worry about the outside world and its affairs. I hesitantly and somewhat reluctantly walk over to his rock and begin to circle it, tracking left as he's told me to do. He cracks one eye at me slightly and seems to smirk. His face softens and I swear I hear him chuckle to himself. "Skye?" he hums sleepily. I stop walking and turn toward him, anxious to hear what he has to say. "You can get back any way you want. There's no ritual to it."

At this, he opens both eyes, lifts his head gingerly from his paws, and winks at me. Then, without changing his self-satisfied facial expression, he closes his eyes again and returns to visit the chambers of his deepest dreams. I can't help but grin. The crazy bastard.

I take one last look at Aglaea, in all her glory. *What's this?* I squint and take a few steps forward to get a better look, and out of nowhere, someone has carved a quotation into her trunk. Must be his work... I look over my shoulder to be sure Lazarus isn't snickering at me again, then I read the words inscribed on Aglaea out loud to myself:

> "Return me to my bane,
> O guard...
> For my Half calls to me.
> Though in the end,
> I'll favor
> Sole confidence in thee."

Part III

"One who has unreliable friends soon comes to ruin, but there is a friend who sticks closer than a brother."

—Proverbs 18:24 (NIV)

It's the next morning of whatever day it is. *Damn, what day is it?* I rub my eyes sluggishly and turn on my bedside lamp to sweep away the darkness of my windowless cell. The moment its rosy light hits the far left corner of the room, I see an enormous animal sitting there behind the door staring back at me.

"What the—?!" I scream, and then I think. *Lazarus.*

At my cry, he jumps slightly.

"Skye, what in blazes are you yelling about?" He asks, looking genuinely confused. *Oh, you know, an oversized, predatory fleabag in your hospital room isn't exactly typical.* "No need to be so harsh," Lazarus responds coolly, scratching the back of his ear. Apparently, I have a talking philosopher-wolf named after a living dead guy following me around...and now he reads my mind.

"Well, sorry, but what are you doing here? And when the *hell* did you start hearing my thoughts?" At this, he laughs. Keeping such a regal composure even in humor, he no less than amazes me. It makes me wonder how he isn't tagging along with someone a little classier than me.

"Skye, all guardians possess the ability. I only had to connect with you for the first time to be able to. One can consider that a carefully thought-out precaution taken by our Creator; if we could try to force our way into humans' minds, we would make them fearful of communication with us. Plus, then we would also be as commonly known as a bedtime story, which would lessen our ability to bring about change and create a negative perception of the Order among the general population." As he finishes, his ears perk up suddenly and his head snaps toward the door. I strain my ears, but hear nothing. "Someone's coming. We'll finish this conversation when night falls once more."

Before I can get another word in, Lazarus vanishes into thin air, leaving no traces of his presence. The door handle turns. I frantically fumble with the lamp's switch and turn it off. Its warmth is not for the frostbitten.

"How are you doing this lovely morning, Skye?" The teal woman chirps, her sharp-edged voice causing me to flinch. It's so unlike Lazarus' voice—so constant, so tranquil. Hers sounds more like a violin—still a glorious noise, but unsettling and tiresome. Its sweetness I've finally figured out…it calls to mind the taste of lemonade with a bit too much sugar, the way it engulfs your senses and as you swallow, it leaves you in need of a glass of water just to dilute the concoction in your stomach.

"Oh, I'm alright. Hangin' in there," I answer halfheartedly, putting on a phony smile. Judging by the expression on her face, she is completely fooled.

"How wonderful! I might just bring in the doctor to see you today!"

"Sounds great, Sugar. Hey, when exactly am I gonna be off my morphine?" At this, she looks me over briefly. She seems to contemplate in her head.

"Well, you sure do look better. If you're feeling fully alert and your pain's starting to fade, I'd say we could start weaning you off it today." *Freedom!* I can hardly believe what I'm hearing. I have no idea how many days, weeks, or months I may have been here, but whatever the number, it's been too long. Getting off morphine will signal the beginning of my fast track out of here, and I'm elated at this news. *I can't wait to tell Lazarus…*

"No need, Skye, no need! Exaggerate your recovery and we'll be out in no time!"

Laz?

"Yes?"

You're starting to creep me out. Thoroughly.

"My apologies. I'll work on that."

Part IV

"But if anyone walks in the night, he stumbles, because the light is not in him."

—John 11:10 (NESV)

Crafty witch must have fed more into me…

The teal woman has changed the fluid in my IV and initially agreed to mix in just enough morphine to ease my pain rather than destroy my awareness, but judging by my inability to even predict what time it is, she gave me the full amount. The only clue I get by surveying my surroundings is the fact that the horrible ceiling lights are off, which means that it's probably between 11:00 pm and 6:00 am.

"Excellent observation, Skye. My best guess is that it's about 2:40 am."

I nod with a smirk, wondering if Lazarus will ever sleep again. For some reason I'm not quite certain of, I reach my right arm over my body to switch on my secret fantasy lamp. Its familiar embrace fills my tender body with relaxation. I sigh. *Better than morphine.*

I hear an echo of my own content soul in my head and can't help but smile.

"Can you feel that, Laz?" I whisper aloud, momentarily carefree. I hear hysterical, yet perfectly sane laughter and know it's him giving me a resounding yes. *Alright, Lazarus. I'm going in.*

"I must admit, I was just beginning to get used to 'Laz'... Wait—going where?"

This is where I feel as though Lazarus has taken all my previous sanity for himself, because in all perfect honesty, I can think of no explanation for him. I chuckle uncontrollably. *I have no idea.*

With this, I gradually sit myself upright and rise from my bed as quietly as possible, subconsciously fearing what may happen if I'm discovered. I quickly shift my eyes toward my nightstand for some kind of light I can carry once I venture out of my room. The teal woman, ever predictable, has of course left me a third source of light, in the form of a small scented candle and a half-empty box of matches. The candle is a pale purple color, almost like the sky in Lazarus's homeland. I snatch it from the miniscule table and hold it to my nose. *Lavender.*

"Ahh, the official scent of the bed-ridden..."

I roll my eyes in agreement. Then it hits me... I am standing up, walking around, and using faultless coordination, with little more than a sharp headache. *And no IV attached.* I nearly panic as I whip around toward my bed again, searching for the stand or an IV line on the floor. *I must have dropped the damn thing standing up.* However, to my surprise, I find nothing. I glance at all four of the room's corners and come to the conclusion that I am not on an IV after all.

"Well that's sketchy."

Yeah, tell me about it. Let's get the hell out of this room.

"Lead the way, partner."

Wait... did I hear you say "sketchy" a second ago?

"Don't blame me, it's common for a guardian to begin to take on his partner's personality once they connect. Nothing I can do there."

A bit chilled, I strike a match with the ferocity of feline claws on sandpaper. I set flame to the virgin wick of the candle and anxiously slide through my door, trying to open it as little as physically possible. I turn to my right and nearly run into a wall. Now I'm a bit disoriented. *Because everyone wants a little Winchester mystery in their hospital!*

The next thing I notice, as I step in the opposite direction, is that the floor creaks. *Is this...* I hold the candle closer to the floor. *...hardwood?* I shift my attention to the walls as I walk one foot in front of the other down this uncomfortably narrow hallway. What seem to be family photos practically wallpaper the left side of the hall. As I hit the end of the hallway, I'm greeted by another bizarre finding—stairs. In shock now, I hesitantly make my way down, my pulse quickening with every step. I reach the bottom and feel the frigid smoothness of marble beneath my feet. I struggle to make out an indiscernible pattern in the beautiful marble floor space, but it covers too much area and the meager light from the candle is not enough to reveal all of it at once. My breathing grows erratic, but I cannot turn back. I've come too far already.

A grand fireplace off to the right of the staircase catches my eye. I hobble over to it, fixated like a madman. More framed pictures decorate the mantle, but there's one I can't look over. It's turned over so it lies face down, as if someone is trying to hide it out of shame. Feeling pity for this poor forsaken relic, I gently prop it back up. And try as I might, I can't stop staring.

This photo depicts a flawlessly beautiful girl, probably about nineteen in this picture, with wildly layered, perfectly groomed hair the color of mahogany and eyes that gleam like jade. The few freckles that tickle her nose draw a refreshing air of innocence about her. She is fair-skinned, wearing a flannel with rolled-up sleeves and sitting atop a magnificent buckskin horse. Her sunny smile brings an ache to my heart, and I can only blindly ponder why there are no other photos of such a chipper and lovely young woman adorning this mantle. She makes the others seem drab, after all. *I wonder how long I've been down here…*

"Too long, Skye. I don't like it."

Ignoring him, I slowly hold the candle up to each individual photo, reassuring myself that the girl is in fact the finest one of them all.

"Skye!" A tone of desperation is in his voice.

And then mental silence.

Lazarus?

"CURIOSITY KILLED THE CAT, MISTER BRAXTON, CURIOSITY KILLED THE CAT!" a ghoulish voice cackles. I jump at the harsh change in sound, shaking out the flame of my candle, and I feel a cold sweat creeping up through my flesh at this familiar breath of insanity. I start to feel lightheaded. *Ah, shit.*

Maniacal laughter cuts in, so loud and echoing that I'm sure it's going to call attention. I glance around frantically, unable to see anything with the candlelight gone. I turn to my right, where it seems darkest. I can feel my pulse quickening with every breath. I squint into this darkness and suddenly the laughter stops. All at once, not ten feet from me, a pair of animalistic eyes glares back at me through the night. The creature meows at me discontentedly.

Lazarus… I'm starting to get a little freaked out here… Where the hell are you?

"Skye! Right here! Come now—this way!"

Lazarus stands where I came from, at the foot of the stairs. He gestures toward the top with his head. “Skye, we haven’t much time. I’ve been scoping the place out for you, and I think someone’s awake. Make much more noise and no doubt they’ll hurry this way,” he explains anxiously.

“Dammit,” I say under my breath. Keeping the cat’s eyes in my peripheral, I cautiously shuffle in Lazarus’s direction. When I notice that it follows me, I stop. It stops.

“It seems to only want to stay a certain distance from you,” Lazarus notes. “Like a little spy from Hell. In any case, let’s go. It obviously won’t get any closer and therefore can’t cause any harm, so if we get back up to the room it should give up.”

I nod and follow his lead up the stairs, hearing that eerie meow just behind me the whole time. I don’t admit it to Lazarus, but I am terrified. My heart is in my throat and I feel adrenaline pulsating through my system. I nearly trip several times due to my poor night vision, until Lazarus offers to let me hold on to his tail. I let him guide me up and we start back down the hallway, but still I hear the cat right behind me. Almost at the room, I feel as though all the pictures on the walls that I can no longer see are frowning at me, saying, “He’s an outsider.”

“The door, Skye! The door! Come on!” Lazarus

growls. I fumble with the door handle, cursing at my shaky hands, and let myself and Lazarus inside, being careful to shut out the cat. It continues meowing after I close the door in its face. I hurriedly get back in bed, placing the candle just where it was on my table. I pull the covers up to my chin, but my eyes refuse to shut. The meowing persists. I take several deep breaths, but by now my heart is racing, probably at an unhealthy rate.

"Ignore it, Skye… If someone comes in here and finds you all hopped up like this, things will take a turn for the worst," Lazarus warns, sensing my fear. He curls up on top of my feet in hopes of calming me.

The meowing stops and is replaced by scratching at the bottom of the door. Lazarus says not another word, and I can tell he's trying to set an example by keeping his eyes closed like he's asleep, but he cannot hide the fur bristling up all down his back. His lips slowly start to curl and I can feel the rumble of a low growl in his throat. He stealthily creeps over to the door and waits. The cat finally reaches its entire paw under the door and scratches the floor, only to have Lazarus snap it with his powerful jaws. The cat tries to tug its paw away, but Lazarus holds it for a few seconds and twists his head sideways before letting it go, ensuring the cat is in agony. We both hear it hiss and yowl briefly before it decides that retreat is necessary. Lazarus snarls through the crack under the door one last time to warn it off, then licks his lips and trots back over to me. His rage has caused him to pant slightly.

"Skye, listen to me. That little imp shouldn't bother you anymore. He's the least of my worries. What I am worried about is where we are. In case you haven't put the pieces together yet, we are not in a hospital. We are in a *house*. There are no other 'patients' here; like I said, I've got everything scoped out. This is someone's home. I have no clue whose, but it leaves a bad taste in my mouth, and it isn't the cat blood I'm talking about," Lazarus says. He cocks an ear back toward the door. "I don't have much time," he continues. "People are stirring. Perhaps they have no suspicions yet, but I can't be in here anyway."

He puts his front paws up on my bed and looks me in the eyes with full intensity. "Trust *no one*, Skye. You are in *danger* here." With that, he vanishes and I feel his presence occupy my mind once more. At this point, I am so overwhelmed that I give up panicking. I no longer fight the exhaustion barred by adrenaline and fall into deep sleep. Or maybe I pass out. I'm not sure which.

Part V

"But I say to you, do not resist the one who is evil. But if anyone slaps you on the right cheek, turn to him the other also."

—Matthew 5:39 (ESV)

Sweet, sweet nothing envelops my mind. The refreshing blankness of a dreamless night fills me. And then it happens. While the canvas of my mind remains bare, I feel the sensation of pressure on my chest. *I'm gonna have a heart attack and die right here.* However, this pressure isn't coming from within me. All at once, it shifts. The terror of last night starts to seep back into me. *Wait a second…*

It is then that I notice that with every shift of this pressure, it seems to shift in four different places. When I feel retractable claws tickling me along with each movement, I jolt awake.

There is nothing on top of me. I look to my left and am a bit startled to see a strange man of about six foot eleven sitting on a stool and reading one of the books from my bedside table. He seems to have missed my jumping awake, so I hold my breath and look down at my arm. I'm hooked up to a drip. *Was last night all just a dream?* The grizzly bear of a man finally notices I'm awake and stands up to his full height, complete with broad shoulders and tree trunks for arms.

"Morning, Braxton. How'd you sleep?" Hulk asks.

"Fine," I respond flatly. He takes a few steps in my direction, and then pauses to glance at my candle, the wick now an obvious black.

"Like lavender, do you?" he questions. His eyebrows twitch slightly.

"The official scent of the bed-ridden, ain't it?" I answer in typical smartass fashion. He chuckles without smiling. When he whips out a clipboard, I finally understand who he is. "Are you my—"

"Doctor, yes. And I'd like to go over something with you, if you don't mind," he says. Something in his voice makes me uneasy.

"Sure. Hey, Doc, first I wanna ask you when I'm gonna be off morphine. The teal—uh, your nurse said I could be weaned off the stuff by now… so why hasn't that happened?"

At this, he storms even closer to me until he's looming over my bed. I see some kind of flame in his eyes, as if he resents me and every word I've said. He grabs me by the shirt and lifts me halfway out of bed, then checks himself.

"Listen, Braxton. I will keep you on morphine as long as I see fit. At the moment, you need it more than you know," he responds, exhaling slowly.

"I don't need it for shit! What is it doing for me besides turning me into some kind of junkie? Not a damn thing! Who do you think you—?!"

All at once, with a vicious swipe of Hulk's hand, I hear the sound of flesh brought down on flesh, and my head swings toward the other side of the room. A full-grown man has just slapped me clean across the face. Half in shock, I slowly turn my head back around to look up at him and notice the teal woman standing horrified in the doorway. She has one hand over her mouth, while the other carries my breakfast.

"Hey, Sugar. You just leave that right here for me. I'm starving. Your friend here is one hellofa guy," I say casually, dismissing the tense atmosphere. Shortly after, my breath catches and it becomes obvious that I'm not feeling quite as indifferent as I sound. I swallow shortly, not as quietly as I intended to, and take one last look up at the Hulk with a smirk. "So," I cock my head slightly. "You were saying?" I go right ahead to my breakfast, reasoning to myself, *Hey, the guy's already slapped me. I think I've quite literally faced enough humiliation to deserve my own damn food.* Hulk waits for the teal woman to exit the room before he speaks again.

"Y'know, Skye, I'm not too happy," he begins. "I'm starting to wonder what thoughts are crossing your mind, and I have to say that I liked it much better when I only had to wonder *if* any thoughts were crossing your mind."

I stop chewing on my piece of toast all at once, debating whether or not to say something.

"Hold your tongue, Skye. Don't you dare piss off that ape again, or so help me Great One..."

It's all I can do not to laugh at this, and Hulk doesn't seem to appreciate the slight trace of a smile adorning my face. He leans over me once more, no doubt trying to appear menacing. "Y'see, Braxton... ideas are the downfall of innocent men. Because once a man gets an idea in his head, he ain't an innocent man anymore. Now," he brings his ugly face close enough to mine for me to bite his nose clean off, "he's a dangerous man." He backs away slowly and holds his hands behind his back, then starts to pace at my bedside as he continues: "And a dangerous man, Skye, is not only a danger to himself..." he pauses with a grimace. "...But a danger to others. You catch my drift, Mr. Braxton?"

I nod, my eyes narrow and searching.

"Glad we understand each other," he replies to my gesture with a wink. "Get some sleep, unless you want the morphine to do that for you." He walks toward the door.

"No rest for the wicked," I finish as he opens it, disgust and defiance on my tongue.

He says nothing in reply, but stops to return my hard stare before finally slipping out the door. I don't break my glare until I can no longer hear his footsteps down the hall.

Part VI

"But of the tree of the knowledge of good and evil you shall not eat, for in the day that you eat of it you shall surely die."

—Genesis 2:17 (ESV)

I bring myself to shut my eyes for a while, relaying what happened in my head. Lazarus keeps himself quiet and doesn't attempt to intervene in my thinking, and eventually I am able to doze off of my own accord. Seemingly upon closing my eyes, I find them opening again. I look down and see my bare feet beneath me as I stand in a familiar coolness. Tall grass pokes up between my toes, and I smile faintly at its tickle. My heavy heart soars as I gaze skyward and find just what I needed to—purple as far as the eye can see.

To my left is Aglaea, and just to her right, Lazarus sleeps atop his rock. The beautiful sight draws a sigh from within me, but now I remember the horse that I confronted the last time I was here. I set my sights on the horizon and, sure enough, recognize its disturbing figure staring back at me. I quickly make my way over toward Lazarus, keeping an eye on the equine terror at all times.

Even as I loom above him, Lazarus remains in a perfectly restful and unsuspecting state. It almost makes me wonder how the world can be such a cruel place, but then I remember that the world is a place separate and distant from here. I decide to sit down beside him, my back resting on the rock. Now it's my turn to watch over him.

I stare at the solitary golden horse in the distance, reassuring myself it will not approach so long as Lazarus is right here. I turn around to take one more look at the great wolf as he sleeps. I can't help but grin at his soft snoring and gently stroke one of his paws.

"Why is it that you treat your mighty guardian as a pet, fool?" a sly voice asks from just in front of me. I whip back around and feel my heart skip a beat when I find the horse standing practically above me, just a few feet away. I calm my rapid breathing and shake my head.

"I don't treat Laz like a pet," I answer shortly.

"'Laz?' You've lowered his dignity to the point of presenting him a nickname?" it asks, its voice heavy with disapproval. Lazarus stirs in his sleep.

"What of it? I respect him all the same, and he knows that," I continue at a whisper. "And it's better than no name, Horse." It stares at me for a moment. It seems more troubled than anything else.

"Very well, Skye," it continues as it dips its head a bit. "My name is Judas. It is my fascination to make your acquaintance here in the Guard Realm."

"We aren't friends, Judas," I state with furrowed brows. He snorts softly and breaks eye contact to glance at the ground.

"I suggested no such thing," Judas contends. "I merely seek an answer to this last question, if you shall permit me to ask."

I nod thoughtfully. "Go ahead."

"Answer me this then…why is it that you seem to be so fond of such a strange beast, and one so different from yourself?" I consider his question for a long minute.

"I guess he's proven himself a good friend and protected me from my own curiosity; I'd trust him with my life," I answer half to myself.

Judas seems relieved at my answer, and as he closes his eyes and sighs to himself, a peculiar breeze sweeps the ground. It upsets the stillness of the area and carries so much presence I feel as though another guardian has come to join us. The stream of air curves up toward Judas and blows his mane straight back. I notice then that his coat is glowing with a new sheen. He takes a few steps backward and all the tack that he's been forced to carry suddenly falls away from him. All the leather and metal, straps and chains, buckles and hooks hit the ground in a heap, and Judas takes on the energy of a new stallion. The breeze dies down and then stops altogether.

"I humbly offer my gratitude, o child of destiny, for you have freed me from the grip of madness. For many moons have I borne it, but no longer," Judas exclaims. He proceeds to bow so low that his nose rests on the ground.

His outburst awakens Lazarus, who has to double-take when the first thing he sees is me sitting less than ten feet from the previously deranged horse.

"Judas," He snarls as he leaps to his feet. "What is your business here? And damn it, it had better be good."

"Lazarus, my brother—" Judas begins, but Lazarus cuts in.

"How *dare* you retain the audacity to call me 'brother?!'" Judas lowers his head frightfully and appears hurt and confused. Lazarus closes his eyes and turns his head away. "Has the madness sapped your memory so?" he asks in a softer tone.

"Over time, it has taken its toll, Brother," Judas responds sorrowfully.

"Does the name Pallard mean anything to you, Judas?" Lazarus questions.

Judas thinks for a moment, then his eyes widen. "And how about the rest of your name, Judas..." Lazarus looks him in the eyes. "...the Betrayer."

At this, Judas shakes his head and pleads, "No, my brother, you must believe me. The madness, it overtook me. I thought not of anything but myself, but it wasn't my doing, Lazarus. Truly you can understand my anguish, Apple Guardian, and my suffering!"

"*Your* suffering?!" Lazarus roars. "You are the very 'brother' of mine who would have me succumb to a never-ending slumber as a result of your own *selfishness!*" He pauses for breath, for as before, his rage has driven him to pant. "Besides," he leaps down from the rock, "there is madness in all of us. That gives no excuse for a selfish soul to credit his inner defeats to madness." He begins to walk back toward Aglaea. Judas cries out in frustration, and even rears up on his hind legs and swipes at the sky. He then looks back at Lazarus, who sits beside Aglaea defensively. I see torment in Judas's eyes and immediately pity him, but Lazarus's eyes have gone cold.

"Leave me, Judas, Betrayer of the Order. You are not welcome here," he finishes. Judas turns and begins to walk away, but stops after a few steps.

"I loved my partner," his voice breaks here, "and she loved me. And at one point, I dare say you loved me just the same." Lazarus swallows, and I finally recognize pain on his face.

"Aye, Brother," he begins, his voice nearly a whisper. "And at one point, you stabbed both of us who loved you in the backs."

"What was all that about?" I ask Lazarus, who shakes his head.

"Skye, it's a long story with roots dating back to the beginning of time. I'll explain just enough for you to be up to speed."

And so we sit down in the grass in the comfort of Aglaea's shade as he spins me a tale of the Noble Order of the Guard Realm, a group of twelve guardians appointed by the Great One Himself to confer with one another and make decisions regarding the distribution of power within the Guard Realm. He explains to me that a few of them had very specific duties outside of their commitments to their partners. Lazarus, for example, had been essentially assigned the job of watchdog over the Realm's sacred, and at the time, nameless, tree. It bore twelve apples, one for each guardian, the embodiment of temptation for all. It was forbidden fruit, so to speak, and none of the Order was allowed to eat it.

At the single most vulnerable point in the life of a guardian's human partner, that guardian's apple would ripen and fall from the tree. Since all the Order gathered around the sacred tree quite frequently in those days, when each guardian's fruit fell, there was typically no trouble with giving in to the alluring temptation—they all supported each other and kept each other away from their fruit, their weaknesses.

Judas was beginning to have an issue with his partner one day. She fell off the buckskin's back while they were having a ride, and the next time she rode him she refused to trust him the way she had before the fall. He was hurt by this, and didn't understand that humans need time to conquer their doubts (doubts being something guardians do not have). Her nervousness made him nervous, and within the week, they were a skittish horse and fearful rider. In her fear, she acquired a new set of tack for Judas in hopes of keeping him under control. She rode him with a harsher bit, a set of draw reins, a martingale to keep his head down, everything under the sun, all the while telling Judas, "Trust me." Guardians, when restrained to the point where they are no longer able to protect, but only to be controlled, lose a certain spark in their spirit. They are then able to doubt, to second-guess, to cower, and to defy.

Judas had enough one day about a month later, and after believing his partner for so long, he finally asked himself why he should trust her when she refused to trust him. His partner, of course, was young and stupid, but he could no longer see that. He threw her out of the saddle and took off without looking back. Sometime afterwards, when Judas was no longer with her, she experienced the most vulnerable moment in her life. This sent the apple specified for Judas falling to the ground. Normally, when a guardian refused his or her apple, it would quickly rot away. However, it happened for Judas when no one except Lazarus stood by the tree. With no partner to live for anymore, Judas's temptation overwhelmed him.

"Unfortunately, I wasn't strong enough to fend him off, nor was I eloquent enough to talk him out of the fatal attraction. The two of us had once been the closest of friends, and honorary brothers of the Order, but that day he blindly cast me aside and left me broken and bleeding at Aglaea's base. That day the fruit sealed insanity within the tack that had already been constricting him like some kind of accursed straitjacket. And on that day, the Order deemed me incapable of guarding the sacred tree and thus cast me into a deep sleep, only to be awakened when my destined partner needed me most."

"And that, Skye, is where you come in," he finishes. It all makes sense now. The tack falling off, the absence of a rider, the "brother" nonsense…

"So," I ponder, "If he gained the ability to doubt and rise up because this girl was pulling back on him too hard, doesn't that mean there's at least some truth in what he says? Didn't that weaken his will?"

Lazarus faces me. "Skye, there is some truth in everything. The saddest truth is, both the Great One and Judas's own partner would have grown to forgive the poor fool for his wrongdoings, had he not succumbed to the forbidden fruit's pull. Judas had a choice in that. Doing what was right might have been made much more difficult for him than for the others, but it was perfectly possible, and his crime was unforgivable."

"His punishment since has been solitude. He's been stripped of his ability to ever become a guardian again, and so he lives a meaningless life here within the Guard Realm. He's been given the names Betrayer of the Order, the Betrayer, and the Deserter. The Order has moved their capital far from here and I am more or less a misfit, bound by my loyalty to the Great One here upon the patch of ground Aglaea shelters, to perform my appointed duty until my last breath leaves my lips."

"And your name…" I say, noticing that Lazarus's eyes are tearing up.

"Allows them to mock me for eternity—the Apple Guardian," he finishes, a single tear gliding down his regal face. And in that moment, I realize that I respect Lazarus more than any man I've ever known.

Part VII

"You will not fear the terror of the night, nor the arrow that flies by day, nor the pestilence that stalks in darkness, nor the destruction that wastes at noonday."

—Psalm 91:5-6 (ESV)

I fall asleep curled up next to Lazarus in the Guard Realm. Finally I am able to sleep with a blank mind. And now begin the nightmares.

I hear a piercing scream that sends chills down my spine. It is the cry of a girl, and it possesses the shrill innocence of youth. The most unsettling thing about this sound is that I know I've heard it before. The curse of familiarity makes me want nothing more than to not have to hear it anymore.

"JP, *wait!*" it calls with discernible words this time. An image of a beautiful rural home nestled in rolling hills flashes through my mind. I can see my breath. The night is black. The scene fades out. "Skye, what the hell are you doing?! Get up!"

I see the frantic face of a young man—a friend. He looks at something to the left, and then runs. I see blood. It's everywhere. Where did it come from? What have I done?

I hold someone in my arms. Her pants are at her ankles, but her struggle is over. She doesn't move. My breathing grows labored. *What have I done?* Again a blood-curdling scream cuts through the darkness in my mind. The smell of gardenia flowers, though faint, envelops my senses.

What have I done?

Part VIII

"And all the men of Israel, when they saw the man, fled from him, and were sore afraid."

—1 Samuel 17:24 (KJV)

I open my eyes. *Damn, I actually slept. What time is it?*

"I wouldn't say you slept well though—didn't quit your mumbling all night. It's quite late in the morning, Sleeping Beauty."

Yeah, yeah, get off me.

"Well fine then, mind yourself; here's Johnny!" I'm about to ask when the hell he got the chance to watch all these movies when the door handle clicks. I jump slightly and watch it turn.

"Good day, Mr. Braxton," a deep, smiling voice sounds as Hulk walks in.

"Morning," I return shortly. Lazarus growls.

"So have you even noticed we've been weaning you off morphine, as you asked?" I quickly look at my wrist and find no IV. *Just like the other night…*

"Yeah, actually."

"Oh," the doctor replies. He tries to sound impressed but I can tell he isn't surprised. "Well fantastic then. You'll be out of here in no time." His eyes gleam, and I shudder at the sudden sound of meowing outside my door. Hulk lets it continue for a moment while staring at me, and I begin to wonder if I'll even make the rest of the day alive. My heartbeat quickens ever so slightly, and I wonder, as I can feel it pulsing in my head, if he can hear it too. Then, just like before, two entire black paws, claws extended, reach under the door, one of them bandaged. I feel sick to my stomach.

Hulk glances over at the door finally, as if he's just noticed, and grins. "You know, Skye, I made the strangest discovery the other day… Our cat, you see, she's not an outdoor cat. She plays, eats, and sleeps in the house. And yet, I found that some sort of large animal has mangled one of her paws. Found bite marks and all," he pauses, brows furrowed, then looks back at me. "Well, you know what they say… Curiosity killed the *cat*." He places an accidental emphasis on "cat," and I start to panic. I swallow hard, trying not to make a sound. The doctor leaves the room then, shooing the cat ahead of him.

I'm going to die here, Lazarus. I'm going to die. I process all the information the doctor has relayed to me, and confirm my fear that he knows exactly how much I know. He knows that I'm aware of my surroundings—

that I'm not in a hospital. He knows something attacked his cat, but does he know about Lazarus?

"Don't worry, Skye, there's no way that could be true. It's impossible."

But I can feel hesitance in his voice. "Anything's possible," I whisper tiredly. "Laz, I can't do this. I don't know what the hell's going on, my head hurts like nobody's business, I mean… Shit, I don't even know why I'm *here!*" For the first time since the death of my grandmother four years ago, I feel the back of my throat ache and nostrils flare. I blink, and all at once I'm crying like I'm nine. Of course, I have no real idea what true suffering is. Everyone's grandparents die at some point. So do everyone's parents, sons, daughters, nephews, nieces, and grandkids. For all I know, I could be lucky. Maybe it's even lucky that I don't know what's going on… That way I don't have to see the darkness looming from the eye of the storm.

"Don't worry. We're going to find out, and we're going to find out tonight."

What?

"Quit crying, you marshmallow, and save some energy. Tonight, we're going nocturnal again."

But—

"Mister Skyyyye," that good old, smoother-than-silk voice rings out as the teal woman bursts in the door. She excitedly drags in some sort of equipment from the hallway. A decent-sized piece of machinery rests atop the cart she rolls towards me, and I look it over curiously. There are probably fifty switches on the thing, but they're off to one side so I can't read what they're for. The teal woman begins to rant wildly about how remarkable this device is and how it'll end my pain for good, and then wraps my hands with sketchy-looking straps. *Wait…are those…* I'm interrupted as she sticks the tip of a wire just into my skin.

A cord hangs from my hands, and leads straight to the machine. At this point, the teal woman dips her head at me slightly, avoiding eye contact. When she backs out of the room slowly and I hear heavy, lumbering footsteps down the hall making the floorboards creak and Lazarus's hackles rise, I understand. The doctor walks in, hands behind his back nonchalantly.

"I thought I'd try a bit of experimental treatment on my best patient," he says, and if looks could kill, I'd have been cold by the time he walked in. He quickly approaches the machine, before I can protest, and flips a switch towards the left of it. Electricity jolts through my body, sending my heartbeat straight to my head. I jump, more from the start than the pain.

"Who…" I start to say as he lets off the switch, but he flicks the switch two to the right of the first. The same sensation fills me once more, but it's amplified to a point that makes me clench my teeth. The bastard holds it there until it gets a grunt out of me, and then lets go. "…the *hell*, do you think you are?"

I am immediately answered with a shock at least six times greater. Now I can hear myself groaning, feel the mock paralysis, see the veins on my arms bulging almost to bursting. My pulse grows faster and heavier, and I'm almost convinced now that it's my brain beating instead of my heart. He lets off, his facial expression unchanging.

"I'm sorry, Skye. What was that? I'm afraid I didn't hear you," he says simply. Between gasps for air, I glare at Hulk, fire in my eyes and murder in his.

"Oh yeah," I return, pretending I'm about to show him respect. "Here, I'll try again: I said, *who the* ***fuck*** *do you think you* ***are****?!*" Sure of my imminent death, I scream this last sentence in his face, my overgrown hair whipping like a madman's. Sure enough, the next shock is excruciating. I cry out in agony, but at the same time my anger meets my terror and comes out sounding frustrated. I thank God that my anger prevents me from fully showing the unbearable pain I'm in. Now all I'm starting to see is light. I hear the buzz of the machine, still on and still merciless, but it seems to grow distant as the image fades out. *This is the end then… I'm dead.*

I open my eyes and the lights are off. I go to scratch my face and find that my hands are strapped tightly to the sides of my bed. After a moment of thought, I panic. *Lazarus.*

Are you okay? Please, for the love of God, tell me you're fine…

"Far from 'fine,' Skye, but so are you, and we'll just have to make do, won't we?"

"Alright, lights are out, that means it's prowling time. Right?"

"Now you've got the idea," Lazarus responds from beside me. He jumps up onto my bed and licks my face. "Now, to get these pesky things off…" With this, he grabs each strap between his teeth and tugs with all his might, making short work of them. I gratefully scratch behind one of his ears and feel around on the nightstand for matches. I strike one against the wall and light up my lavender candle. I grab two extra matches, just in case I lose my flame, and stick them in the otherwise useless pocket of my hospital getup. After picking up the candle, I turn back to Lazarus, who seems in the same mood as I.

"We'll show this bastard," we say as one, hearts on fire.

Part IX

"Blessed are the pure in heart, for they will see God."

—Matthew 5:8 (NIV)

I tread lightly as I step into the hall, Lazarus shadowing just behind. I can tell by his obvious intensity that he's having trouble keeping himself from growling. We move together in harmony, as any fine team. Once we reach the stairs, he's at my side, his loyal and protective instinct taking over. I grin viciously as I take the first step. We make quick work of the staircase, focused only on our mission. Sure enough, when I frantically search the fireplace mantle for the fantasy girl, her picture is again turned down. This time, I grab the small, framed photo and shove it in my pocket. Lazarus keeps watch for me. I then gesture for him to follow me back upstairs. Though confused at the short amount of time I've taken, he neither doubts nor questions my judgment.

We reach the hall and again the strange faces twist at us…always frowning, always watching. I examine these photos more closely and a placard on the wall catches my eye:

In loving memory of Taylor Jane Pallard
1993—2013
We will never forget.

"Shame," I remark. "What a short life."

"They do say that only the good die young, don't they?" Lazarus points out, staring intently at the placard. I shrug, half-nod, and continue cautiously toward my room. Once behind a closed door, I sit down on my bed and pull out the photo. I switch on my lamp and the whole room feels warmer. The rosy light has become my security blanket. It brings a smile to my face as I stare at this mysterious girl with relish. Her soft features are nothing like the life I live now—so sharp, so cold; mine is a world of concrete and ice. After soaking in the tranquility of the night for some time, I'm reminded of Aglaea and the Guard Realm. I look at Lazarus, dozed off next to me on the bed, and chuckle to myself. I rub behind one of his ears tenderly and he turns to me.

"Alright, Lazarus. Time for bed," I murmur, longing for the peaceful silence to never end. Sensing this, he simply nods at me with soft, smiling eyes.

"Sleep, Skye. I shall see you quite soon, I think, within the Guard Realm."

"Yeah," I answer sleepily. "Count on it."

Slowly, I feel the presence of Lazarus fill me up from the inside out, casting a ray of drowsiness upon me. I reach over reluctantly and shut off my lamp. My eyelids grow heavy, and finally my world goes black. Once again, I can smell the green of grass surrounding me. I shift my bare feet in its plush coolness and feel the warmth of natural light on my face, a feeling I suddenly realize I haven't known in some time. Without thinking, I dive into the grass, its blades shivering around me. I bury my face in its fresh embrace; the pure, earthy smell of life engulfs me. I feel alive again. It is when I begin to laugh out loud in joy that I notice a condescending beast, daintily crossing its paws and watching my every move with smiling eyes.

"Having a good time, are ya?" Lazarus asks, every fiber of his being spelling his amusement.

"Oh, Laz," I laugh, "How could I not? It is a beautiful place you oversee, oh most noble guardian—" Lazarus leaps from his rock and pounces on me playfully. I can hear him growling in glee. We roll over each other a few times, all in good fun.

Lazarus pauses for a moment, in full play-bow, and I catch a glimpse of what his life could be like, without me in it. Without some troublesome human to babysit, he could be spending all of his days bathing in the sunlight; he could be rolling in the grass, or perhaps even still palling around with Judas. And as I look into his eyes in this brief moment, I see the dilated pupils of a feisty young pup—no less and no more. His tail is lifted and wagging, and I feel a pang of pity for my friend Lazarus…for he has never known the carefree life of a brilliant hunter of the wild, has never been able to simply do as he pleased, and has never had companionship with others of his kind.

I have a responsibility to this truly amazing creature. While he carries the burden of guardianship, I should be the one to remind him that he is a part of myself, and therefore doesn't always have to fix the mistakes I make. Until now, I've placed too much pressure on him and his judgment. But seeing him now, for not only who he is, but for the first time what he is as well, I silently pledge to myself, within the confines of my own heart, that from now on, we are not a master and an apprentice, but rather a full-fledged duo—a team.

I snap out of this short epiphany to the sound of a joyous yip escaping Lazarus as he bounds toward me again. This time, I make a move. I lunge for him and pin him carefully to the ground, and we collapse in a tangled heap. We laugh in unison, raising a glorious sound while panting like fools. We lie there in the security of Aglaea's shade for what seem like hours, but neither of us says a word or minds. Suddenly, Lazarus jolts to attention.

"The bindings…" he mutters. "The bindings, a-and the photo—I have to go return things to the way they were, or the doctor will suspect something."

I glance at him worriedly. "Is that possible?"

"Skye, you underestimate me yet," he sighs, his mind preoccupied. "Of course. It's possible when you're awake and conscious, and it's no less possible when you're asleep within the Guard Realm." He stands and turns to me. "I'll return shortly. Mind yourself."

I nod, and in one blink, he is gone. I remain where I sit in the grass and search the outfit I'm sporting. I pat all of my pockets and find that something solid is inside one of my coat pockets. I reach inside, and my muscle memory sends chills throughout me. *The photo.* I pull it out, and sure enough, the girl beams back at me, a symbol of simpler times. I sigh faintly and walk to Lazarus's rock to sit down. I am instantly lost in the picture, as I have been each time before, and lose track of time.

"Wh…where did you get this?" an incredulous voice murmurs from over my shoulder. I start at its familiar uncomfortable tone. "What have you to do with my partner? How did you come to obtain this?!"

"What are you talking about, Betrayer?" I answer shortly, brow furrowed.

"That girl, Pallard. She is my partner! I am the very

one she sits the back of in this photo!" he cries out in desperation. My stomach jumps.

"What did you say..?" I begin. Judas simply stares back at me in wonder, as if all the explanation in the world couldn't justify anything going through his mind.

"Answer me, traitor! This girl... did you say her name is Pallard?"

Part X

"He that covers his sins shall not prosper: but whoever confesses and forsakes them shall have mercy."

—Proverbs 28:13 (AKJV)

"How *dare* you rebuke me?" Judas hisses, his eyes narrow. "You should know as well as I that that girl's name is Pallard, criminal!" He begins to tremble, then softens and lowers his gaze. "I am aware of what I've done, and I have paid for my sin every song since." Then he turns once more. "You," he snarls, "you have yet to fathom your sins. The Great One should let you *burn!*" Judas stops himself abruptly. I begin to back away, and when he looks at me with mourning eyes, I turn toward Aglaea. He returns my gesture and lopes off a good distance.

I feel the progressive beat of a great drum sending tightness through my body, and say to no one in particular, "A mighty instrument," I grow short of breath. "One enough to smother…" My train of thought drifts as Lazarus reappears before me.

"Laz, do you think the madness will ever return to Judas?"

"Oh, the poor bastard's mad alright," he snorts, then pauses. "In seriousness, no. It was you who lifted the curse from him, and the Great One has mercy enough to let lifted curses be the end of one's suffering."

"How exactly did I—?"

"You spoke to him words he had long yearned for his partner to speak of him, therefore justifying his frustration. No one else would even consider showing him empathy, and this is why he is so drawn to you," He smiles faintly. "You're a good man, you know. A good man with a mighty heart." I pause. My soul seems to grow heavy as I stare at the ground silently.

"You know, Skye, someone wise once told me this: those bitter will fight; those empty will fall, but it is he of great heart who will salvage them all."

His words turn over in my head for a long minute before I'm reminded of something I've been meaning to ask. "Hey, I've heard you talk about 'songs' as a unit of time before. Does time pass in the Guard Realm, then?"

Lazarus rolls his eyes and answers patiently, "Yes, Skye, of course. Time must pass within any realm, and it does in mine as it does in yours, only differently so." He gestures toward the sky with a nod. "There is no night and day in the Guard Realm, if that's what inspired your question. As for songs...just wait."

I think to ask him more, but control myself and instead sit at peace in the grass. I close my eyes and sigh, drinking in the bittersweet silence. Feeling secure within the Guard Realm for the first time, I lie back in the lush growth. Judas no longer seems a threat, but a tortured soul. Lazarus is no longer a shady figure, but a dear friend. Just as I contemplate dozing, a magnificent sound whistles through Aglaea's limbs, somehow without upsetting her stillness. Not a blade of grass flinches at this phantom breeze, and I can almost hear a melody; a faint song seems to whisper. When I open my eyes, I cannot catch the melody. However, when I close them once more, it hums through my being, bringing life to the drumbeat within me. This shy song of mystery enchants me. It is a joyously tragic melody, a tale of ages past, of eternal love, and of wonder, all told without words. It reverberates through me, consuming my consciousness. Within minutes, this song starts to carry away into the distance, as if it is sweeping over the Guard Realm. I long to open my eyes and chase it far away, but I cannot risk missing even a second of it. When it at last fades from earshot, I feel lighter.

"Ahh," Lazarus whispers, "Thirty songs now, it's been."

He explains to me the approximate time difference between the Guard Realm and the "Half-Realm," as guardians call the tangible, human world. Every two days in the Half-Realm is the equivalent of one "song," the appropriately used guardian term for a year within the Guard Realm. The melody is identical every time, and it marks each new song without fail. As it turns out, the one I got to experience represented the thirtieth anniversary of the day Lazarus and Judas were cast into shame and solitude, and I can see in Laz's eyes the sentimental significance.

"Well," he seems to break away from reminiscing. "Let's be getting to sleep, my friend. It's healthier that you dream." With a nod, I lie back down and shut my eyes. Drowsiness falls over me quickly. It isn't long, however, before the calming blackness of my mind becomes claustrophobic and I can hear shouting similar to what I heard in my dreams several nights ago:

"Skye, let go of her! Get out of there, dammit!"

"You, fucking, idiot!"

The shouts grow more vivid, and to my dismay, the blackness clears. Again, I hold the girl in my arms, and again, her gray sweatpants cover only her feet. I am gasping for air, as though suffocating in regret, as I hold her and hold her. Trembling something awful, I pull a knife from her ribs and squeeze it. I hold it close to my chest and take it all in—the girl's dark hair, her fair skin, and her bleeding body. I turn to pick my belt up off the ground, and then I hear the hysterics.

"What the hell is wrong with you?!"

A woman's chilling scream haunts the background of the shouting.

"*You filthy fucking* rapist!"

The last word sends a ringing to my ears. I begin to stand, still fixing my belt. Clutching the knife with a violently shaking hand, I raise it facing the man running toward me. I can hardly make out faces. As the man approaches, wielding a wooden baseball bat, his face becomes clearer. I know this face... The closer he gets, the more massive he appears. And in a fleeting moment, as the giant man brings his bat down upon me, I catch what the woman is screaming.

"TAYLOR!"

"Skye, calm down," Lazarus insists. "Let's try to be rational here." He sits atop his rock, both of us awake within the Guard Realm once more, as I pace back and forth.

"There's no *way* to be rational, Lazarus! Do you even know what this implies?!" His eyes turn back frantically, revealing his inner doubt and fear. "Laz, I am a *ra*—"

"*Enough*, alright? I get it!" He barks sharply. He

squeezes his eyes shut, torment about him. "I suppose all your skeletons are out of the closet, then," he mutters. Astonishment washes over my aching being at his bizarre words. Never before has his tone seemed so full of accusation. Confusion simmers in my mind until it boils into blindness.

"Y-you," I choke, "you knew about this?" When he offers no response, I persist. "Damn it, Apple Guardian, answer me!"

"*Of course not!* What kind of guardian do you think I *am?!*" he roars. I sigh quickly, half startled and yet relieved. "Well, not entirely, anyway," Lazarus pants. Before I can raise my voice again, he continues, "Look, Skye, your concussion affected me just as it affected you. Naturally, I couldn't remember what you'd done. However, I've had a nagging feeling I'd forgotten something, and it hasn't left me until just now. What even I don't understand, though…" here he pauses and swells with sorrow, his chest filling with air, "…is why."

My heart flutters at this last statement. I know his judgment is implied. That much pains my soul, but can I blame him? I collapse into the grass and bury my face in my hands, tremors tearing over me. At last, it's all there in front of me. At last, all the loose ends have been tied. And at last, I come to terms with what I've done; I realize for the first time since I met Lazarus who I really, truly am—a filthy, fucking rapist. All at once, I hate myself. Judas's words from earlier echo in my mind:

"You should know as well as I that that girl's name is Pallard, criminal!"

Criminal…

"The Great One should let you BURN!"

"BURN!"

Burn!

Burn.

Part XI

"In anger his master handed him over to the jailers to be tortured, until he should pay back all he owed."

—Matthew 18:34 (NIV)

"Return me to my bane, O Guard; for my Half calls to me, though in the end I'll favor," I hesitate as my eyes meet his, "sole confidence in thee." Lazarus sits solemnly on his pedestal without a word, so I turn away from him and close my eyes. When I open them again, they are flooded by disgusting, fluorescent light. I find myself choking awake.

"He's up!" I hear the voice of the teal woman cry. She is sitting so close to my bed that it startles me to see her. Then I hear the four horsemen approaching, pounding down the hallway. The gates of Hell open before my eyes, and the Devil's own torturer is grinning in the doorway with his box of lightning.

"Well," Hulk begins, "then things are certainly about to get interesting." Again, he approaches slowly. He's a lumbering stormcloud, ominous and foreboding. Again, he has the teal woman strap my hands. Again, he sticks me with a wire. Again, fire shoots through my veins; again, I shout in explosive agony. After what seems like an eternity, he rips the tip from my skin and wheels his box of lightning away, temporarily shutting the gates of Hell behind him. The teal woman offers me a small tray of food, evidently forgetting that my hands are tied down.

With sweat running down my brow, I breathe, "Water." She simply stares at me with wide, cow eyes, horror on her face. Her bottom lip quivers as if she's about to cry, and she turns away for a moment. "Water," I persist. "Please." At this, she gives the tiniest shake of her head, keeping one hand curled to her face.

She turns back to face me, and something peculiar happens. The second our eyes meet, she collapses onto the ground in tears, like a bag of sand dropped into a puddle. When she stands and shakily sets the tray in my lap, I remember what it's like to be troubled by mixed feelings; I once more feel the inner turmoil of conflicting thoughts, and the faintest touch of pity comes over me. She releases only my left hand and gestures to the tray, still silent. A good-sized chunk of bread and a small bowl of soup sit neatly on top of a napkin. I close my eyes and exhale, fearful. *That's it, then. In a matter of weeks, I'm gonna die here.*

For the next couple of days, they give me no water

directly. The amount of water in my food decreases day by day, as do the portions of food. It's been at least a week of this. I stare obsessed at the calendar they've pinned to my wall. What's left of my good logic tells me I shouldn't trust the date to be accurate, but I can't help clinging onto the promise of reality. My own sickness festers within me as I lie awake in silence. Weary days and sleepless nights pass as I grow more and more disgusted with myself. I am a coward, refusing to sleep in the night for fear of my recurring nightmare; dreading being struck by my past.

The glow of health has seeped out my pores; the witty glint in my eye is long gone. Every day I closer resemble a corpse, beaten into submission by a gravedigger's shovel. Each afternoon I sit through the frying of my nerves by invisible lightning. In time, I take it with little more than a grimace. I grit my teeth and bear my cross, knowing that no amount of torment, no measure of pain, will ever be able to change my fate. This taste of internal fire is only temporary, but when I'm finally taken, my flames will be eternal.

After managing a few hours of sleep the night before, I awaken to my door swinging open. Hulk strides in with an atypically eager smile, knowing he's early today. I frown at the rolling box he pushes in front of him, as always. Only, this time it's different. I squint at it as he sets it up against the wall facing me and realize it's a television. I blink dazedly. Surely I'm hallucinating; that's been happening a lot lately.

"Skye," Hulk croons mockingly, "Your health—well, er—we've done all we can, truly. At this point, we'd really just like to make you as comfortable as we can, given your, condition. So here," he makes an exaggerated gesture at the TV. "It's got twelve channels!" I'd spit at him, but I don't have the piss and vinegar left in me—or any fluids, for that matter. Hulk tosses me a remote and promptly leaves the room. I stare and stare at the remote in my hand. I run a finger over all the buttons and trace around them twice, marveling at the smooth texture I've grown so unfamiliar with. The ugly gray plastic is as silky to the skin as the teal woman's voice is to the ear—almost. And as I touch the remote, I look up slowly at the calendar above the TV.

"The date," I whisper. I've been made an animal. I do not look forward, because all I can see is death ahead of me. I cannot turn back, because madness lurks ever just behind. I do not search for finer things or simpler times, for these no longer have any part in me. But the *date*, the *date*... "The date," I chant, eyes blank and staring. I fumble with the remote for a moment and turn on the television, flipping through my twelve channels. I quickly find what I'm looking for and gasp.

"Good morning, this is news on 2. The time is now 7:02 on this rainy November 18th, 2013; what's traffic like, John?"

I laugh out loud, overjoyed at being able to watch the news and finally know what time and day it is. However, my happiness is short-lived, as I realize that this privilege can be revoked at any given time. They probably wouldn't like me keeping up with stuff going on outside this room. So, I reluctantly change the channel. I find some mindless sitcom and leave it there just for background noise; I'm awfully lonely.

Hours pass, programs begin and end, and I don't bother to pay attention to what time it is. Hulk returns at his usual time, with his typical box, and I stare with hollow eyes in the same old direction. He sets me up, positions himself behind the lightning box, and pulls up a stool for comfort. His expression as we exchange glances speaks of satisfaction; it declares a sort of solemn pride. He sends the lightning through me, amplified in comparison to yesterday. I writhe and scream, only from reflex. After he holds down one switch for a particularly long time, I shout.

"Is that all?! *More!* Give me more fire! Punish me, dammit! That's all you *got?*" He only sends one more wave through me, then bends down close to my face, unshaven and seemingly sleepless as I. In a tone of mockery, he inquires:

"Do you believe in God, Skye?" I pause for a moment to regather my fried brain, then:

"Sir," my breath catches, "I believe in nothing."

Slowly, my ears begin to ring, the walls around me sway, and I see an impending black fog behind my eyes. I grow suddenly very sick to my stomach, and my head falls back onto my pillow. A rhyme flashes like a warning label across the emptiness of my mind. I whisper it to myself rapidly; inaudibly,

"So day is done, so night has come,
I follow in my sleep
The calling of my Guardian
To a world long obsolete."

Just as the darkness closes in on me, I jolt awake lying in the grass of the Guard Realm. I hear the disturbing sound of quarreling animals and turn around quickly. Under Aglaea I can see three things: Judas, fussing and screaming as horses do when spooked, Lazarus, snarling and bristling beneath him, and the thing no guardian ever wants to see close up—the apple.

Lazarus is in a frenzy, barking madness from his frothing mouth. He runs in distorted circles around Judas, who valiantly stands over the apple. Judas's legs are slashed up and bleeding, the whites of his eyes expressing his unshakeable fear. Unsure of what I should do, and positive I can't fend off a crazed predator, I stand and stare. I try to think, but the detached possession in Lazarus's eyes chills me to the bone. His mighty jaws snap violently at the air as Judas stands on his hind legs and repeatedly slams his front hooves down. Lazarus can only keep a safe perimeter without being trampled.

Finally, Judas notices me. His eyes grow even wider and more frantic. I decide to do the dumbest thing I can possibly do and sprint toward them. Lazarus is too preoccupied to see me coming, so I take a leap of faith and blindside him, clutching the thrashing terror with all my might. His legs flail about as he cries aloud, half howl and half snarl. It's a maniacal sound, and certainly one that should never escape an animal.

I use both arms to keep his head on the ground, covering the rest of him with my body weight. He continues to thrash and strike out with his legs. Struggling, I shout, *"Lazarus!"* For an instant, he seems to recognize my voice and turn it over in his head, but his mind is consumed by the apple's wicked compulsion. "Lazarus, that's enough! Calm down! You don't know what you're doing!"

Judas cries out doubtfully, "You'll have to do a hell of a lot better than that, Skye!"

I curse to myself, then continue, "Laz, buddy—you know me. You can trust me. I trusted you on the first day I came here, didn't I? You had me walking circles around a rock, for God's sake! And you know what? I'd still trust you with my life. I found you on my own time, but you waited here thirty songs for me to wake you up. You must have trusted me an awful lot, the way you were so patient with me back then. With all those stupid questions I asked, with every dipshit call I made; with every awful decision that you could have easily intercepted, you went along for the ride and helped me every step of the way because you *knew* I had a story to live. I dare say you trust me right now, no matter how much you fight me. And I just said I trust you with my life, so you know what? Let's stop this bullshit. We're lookin' pretty medieval here." To Judas's surprise and obvious horror, I slowly release Lazarus and get to my feet. I back up to where Judas stands and assist him in guarding the apple.

Lazarus lies there for a moment, then stands shakily. He starts toward us, convulsing as though we are in the process of performing an exorcism. Judas remains petrified, his nostrils blowing as a weary horse's do. Lazarus looks me in the eye, and I see him in there for a moment as he says, "Skye, thank you," then, something I know instantly I will never forget: "Your story isn't over, and I am honored to have been part of it. I only wish," his body retches, "I only wish I could have seen it through to the end." After this, the fever of madness returns to his eyes. He lunges at Judas, who tries to remain on the defense until Lazarus gets a brutal hold on his leg. Judas cries out in fear and rears up, throwing Lazarus to the ground, and then hesitates only briefly before swinging a hind leg. There's no mistaking—it was a blow for the kill. Lazarus collapses in the grass. The tremendous pain he's in is obvious. He looks up at me one last time, back in his right mind, then closes his eyes and starts to speak softly.

"So day is done, my night has come,
O man to salvage man,
Sole confidence I boast in thee,
In prayers we'll meet again."

We'll Carry On

"Blessed are the poor in spirit, for theirs is the kingdom of heaven."

—Matthew 5:3 (NIV)

The world around me slams to a halt, time hanging frozen in the air like a fog. Neither Guard nor Half Realm exists, not Judas nor Aglaea, nor the purple of the sky, nor the plush of the overgrown grass. All at once, nothing in any of God-knows-how-many worlds and universes matters. All I can see is the frail distortion of my guardian lying at my feet. I kneel down beside him and lean in close, anxiety filling my chest. In fear—desperation—I cry out to him. He opens his weary eyes to meet mine, and I lose my breath. My shoulders heave uncontrollably. I rest a hand on the side of his shoulder and bow my head to keep him from seeing how pathetic I am.

"Lazarus," I breathe, "What am I gonna—" I stop when I look up and find that his eyes, though open, are no longer focused on anything in particular. "...do?" I bury my fingers in his wild fur and scream. I just linger over him, and scream and scream. Quickly enough I run out of energy and vocal stamina and recede into sobbing. I lie over his broken body, inhaling deeply into his fur. "What am I supposed to do without you, Laz? I'm… I'm no good without you. I've done terrible things without you, and I hate me without you. I *need* you."

I close my eyes, my head still resting on my fallen guardian, and focus on controlling my breathing. Words I resented when I was young dance through my mind in wisps: *"Exult O shores, and ring O bells, But I with mournful tread,"* I cannot contain the tightness in my face, for it aches. *"Walk the deck my Captain lies, Fallen cold and dead."*

To my surprise, I am still lying over the great wolf when I awaken. No terrors have consumed me, not a breath of stale Half-Realm air is in my lungs, and all is quiet.

"Skye," comes Judas's voice over my shoulder. "Why are you still here?" I stare blankly ahead and blink, only half aware of his question. "Let him rest, brother. He has found peace; why then can't you?" *Brother.* Something about that echoes into the core of my soul.

"That's what he was to me," I breathe. "He was a brother, a part of me. The *better* part of me. What peace is there for me if that's gone?" Judas lifts his head and gazes at Aglaea's branches for a long time, content to think in silence. I look up at him and, seeing that he's closed his eyes, follow suit. The familiar whisper of the Guard Realm's eerie song surrounds me, a melancholic tone seeming to pervade it this time.

"We are all brothers here, Skye," Judas says softly once the song carries off. "And even I, an ex-guardian, cannot tell you what peace you have yet to find, or where it may lie, or how to discover it. In times of darkness, none of us know where our path will lead. We simply carry on and wait for the dawn to light our way. In the Guard Realm, only figurative darkness exists." He pauses and watches as a faded leaf falls from Aglaea's foliage. Another follows promptly, and yet another after that one.

"Sometimes, I think that is the most difficult darkness to navigate; it is the kind we find within ourselves," he says. His mourning is different—not necessarily detached, but surer somehow. It's as if Judas sees a piece of his own future lying at his hooves, and perhaps he does. Something in his tranquil expression speaks of relief, of an exhaling of burdens, while at the same time showing such deep-rooted sorrow that I can't bear to look at him.

"It's been a song since Lazarus fell, my brother," he says. "The time has come for you to return to your realm. I promise, you shall always carry the Guard Realm within you, and your guardian… He was the finest I have ever known. I have no worry over the fate of his soul. The Great One knows he was a brave soldier for things pure and good, and he never fell to the ultimate temptation. He was…"

"A man of great heart," I finish for him. Judas smiles and a gleam of nostalgia wets his eyes. "I can't come back here again once I leave, can I, Judas…"

"I'm afraid not this time, Half-Brother," he says with a faraway smile. "But as Lazarus said, your story isn't over yet. If it's anything like it has been so far, yours will be a legendary tale." I nod, my attention now introspective.

"Aren't you mad at me?" I finally ask, referring to my history with Judas's partner.

"I suppose I've no further excuse to be; I've taken your guardian from you," he answers, once again watching leaves fall from Aglaea. "But I truly am beginning to believe that things aren't as simple as we think. You're a man of great heart, sharing Lazarus's own fiery soul, and even if you were my Taylor's killer at one point, I see a different man before me now. I could ask nothing more of fate, for even guardians cannot change what has already come to pass." Aglaea catches my eye as leaves begin to fall more rapidly, in such great volumes that they fill the air around us. A breeze rests them over the great wolf where he lies in the grass.

"I knew the Great One had not forsaken him," Judas says with smiling eyes. "Look, even Aglaea mourns her guardian."

"You were the wise one who gave Laz that quote," I say, connecting the dots. He just looks back at me once before turning away. Aglaea's boughs are now bare and somehow still magnificent, even in their emptiness finding beauty. *There's my peace.* I watch Judas depart a final time and decide that it's time I word my own way back.

So day is done, so night has come
I now as I depart
Shall carry my guardian
As he carried me,
And know he's alive in my heart.

I jolt awake to the sound of monitors blaring. *I must have been in a coma.* I can hardly control my breathing, and I watch my chest heave wildly like a trapped rabbit awaiting its demise. No one else is in my room now. I try to sit up, but am too weak from starvation and dehydration. *And of course, again with the damn wrist straps.*

But something occurs to me suddenly. I cannot be

complacent any longer. Lazarus would have found a way out, and I know I can do the same if I muster up even five seconds of strength. I have the heart of a guardian living within me—the heart of the greatest guardian any realm has ever known. I glance around the room, eyes shifting quickly like a feral beast surrounded. I know it's only a matter of time before someone bursts through the door. I spot the TV remote on my bedside table, take a deep breath, and tear my left hand from its binding. I grab the remote and switch on the news, my arm trembling from the sudden effort. I need to know what day it is.

"Breaking news in the Bay Area today, a man by the name of Jared Polinski has turned himself in to local authorities for a crime he says he committed several months ago." My stomach turns immediately. I know that name. *The initials… J.P.*

"Seeing the man was distraught, police held him overnight on suspicion of drug abuse, but he has not changed his position." Something inside me cries out, and I begin shouting at the top of my lungs.

"*Hey!* Hulk, Teal, get your asses in here! I'm awake and getting the hell *out!*" I hear quick, pounding footsteps outside the door and realize what I'm doing is crazy. If this isn't going where I think it's going, it'll all be over for me. But if it is… I'll finally be home free. The two swing the door open, evident surprise painting their faces.

"Skye, why you," Hulk begins, marching toward me with a dead stare.

"Polinski even had names to provide, and was reportedly almost incoherent in his recollection of framing a Mr. Skye Braxton, a friend of his at the time, who has coincidentally been missing for a similar amount of time."

Hulk stops in his tracks. His eyebrows lift, and for the first time since I met him, he looks genuinely human. He turns his full attention to the news, forgetting anyone else is in the room or even exists at all. I can tell he's anxious to hear her name.

"Polinski told authorities that he is responsible for the rape and murder of a Taylor Pallard, a young woman with whom he had reportedly been in a secret relationship. Polinski said that she had recently ended the relationship with the man nearly eight years older than her and that he showed up at her house that evening intending to scare her, but was given to a fit of rage. He even offered an address in the inland hills, and upon confirming the last name of the homeowners, authorities in the area were sent out to the rural property about an hour ago for further investigation. More to come." I turn back and forth between Hulk and the television screen, incredulous.

"I knew it," I say aloud, "I knew I didn't do it!" Hulk says nothing, but I watch as tears stream down his face. In what might be his first display of weakness since I first woke up in this Godforsaken place, he falls to the floor and buries his face in his hands. He and the teal woman are now weeping before my eyes, and I can't help but get choked up myself when I hear sirens outside in the distance. This is it. Lazarus knew all along that it couldn't have been that simple. I know that my quick reaction time was his doing; he's created a fighter in me. I was able to rise to the challenge because I knew that the most vulnerable moment of my life had already passed—the moment I temporarily had no faith in anything. Not in God, not in my guardian, not even in myself. From that moment on, I've known that believing in nothing is not an option. For the sake of my guardian's legacy, I needed to rise from my rock bottom. I had to prove that Lazarus has made me a better man.

Never in my life have I been so happy to hear police kick down a front door. I can hear one, two, three, four, maybe five sets of feet sprinting up the stairs just down the hall.

"Skye, it's a blessing that you've survived all this," Hulk says to me once he is able to quit sobbing. "Words can't describe—"

"It's fine, Doc," I interrupt, my voice trembling. "I wouldn't put anybody in my place, not JP, not even you. I'll pray for your damn psychotic soul every night, man. I've seen Hell, and it ain't a pretty place." He stares back at me for a second before police pour into the room and yell for the two to put their hands up. They comply, obviously bogged down with guilt, and I say nothing further. I know they'll reap whatever consequences they've sown. There's no reason to waste energy agitating their tortured souls; they'll never feel right again after doing what they've done. Their story isn't mine to reflect on.

It all seems surreal as I watch them escorted out of the house in handcuffs. I guess I assumed it would never end, and that I'd die there without a sound. But my story wasn't over. I walk outside after practically being carried down the stairs by officers, my legs barely strong enough to hold me. I stand there for a while, watching the wind move the trees gently. I've forgotten what real trees look like; they're beautiful, but none compare to Aglaea. I stare intently at the fog of my breath in the crisp November air, watching it rise and carry off into the breeze. *Like a song.*

My hands rest in the pockets of the jeans I've been provided, which are comically large for my skeleton-like body. My knuckles and veins jut out like those of a ripe old man, bringing a smile to my face as I poke fun at myself in my head. I look around and examine the long dirt drive, the rolling hills of gold, and the long-neglected front yard. The house is quaint and clean-looking, if a little old. It's an oddly charming setting for the horrors that have taken place within its privacy. Paramedics approach me and begin asking me frantic questions, to which I raise a hand and reply,

"Anyone have a smoke?"

CPSIA information can be obtained
at www.ICGtesting.com
Printed in the USA
FSOW02n0426220816
24022FS

9 781478 778608